PURGING THE MONSTERS

Julie Bloss Kelsey

Purging the Monsters

©2026 Julie Bloss Kelsey
All Rights Reserved

First Printing

ISBN 978-1-970860-03-0

Cover Art Credit: Kawanabe Kyōsai. Kyōsai's Pictures of One Hundred Demons. 1890. The Metropolitan Museum of Art.

CUTTLEFISH
BOOKS

ACKNOWLEDGEMENTS

Grateful appreciation is offered to the editors and publishers of *AlienSkin Magazine, Bleached Butterfly, Cthulhu Haiku II: And More Mythos Madness* (Popcorn Press, 2013)*, dadakuku, Eye to the Telescope, Failed Haiku, #FemkuMag, FOCUS Magazine, Frogpond, Grasping the Fading Light: A Journey Through PTSD* (Sable Books, 2023)*, horror senryu journal, kontinuum, The Math Haiku Project, microcosms, ONE ART Haiku Anthology* (2025)*, Otoroshi Journal, Outshine, Prune Juice Journal, Scifaikuest, Scryptic, Star*Line, tiny frights, tsuri-dôrô, Under the Basho,* and *whiptail: journal of the single-line poem* in which some of these poems have previously appeared or are forthcoming.

this urge to apologize
for things I didn't do...
slow rolling fog

trauma bond—
contagion flowing
from your soul to mine

every morning
his hands tight
around my neck

I can never
scream long enough
to expel you—
echoes of your madness
forever touching me

in a broken mirror
fragments of my younger selves
...fractal moon

the way
your criticism
sticks in my mind...
a mental tapeworm
I extract and burn

smokescreen
my conscience
going up in flames

failing to understand charred roses

wishing I could
save you from yourself—
rising thunderhead

beneath the veneer
of polite society
her visage slithers

insult me again
and I will eviscerate you
such violent thoughts
lurk behind my gentle
quiet smile

waiting for you
to say you're sorry
a death knell

the voice of reason
distorted babbling
in white noise

only one way
to his heart—
sharpening the saw

bloody knife
the gash in his neck
brings me closure

the long bones of her leg honing the blade

peeling back your skin
the expiration date
now clearly visible

family ties—
his billfold sewn
from human skin

unpacking my guilt:
this suitcase full of dirty clothes
and severed limbs

blood bubbles
the bathtub fills
with broken bodies

death watch—
listening to each soft breath
of the wind

waiting for me
on the back porch
blow flies

a spider curls up
in her nasal cavity—
bleached skull

handmade rocking chair—
the creak
of old bones

basalt upthrust
even the reddened sky
an accusation

with every dawn
a new confession...
gone darkside

memories
I need to stay buried—
prison break

falling cards the house panic built me

bad neighborhood—
nails protruding
in my mind

the gunshot
ricocheting inside
my memory

long after midnight
tumbling around in the sheets
negative thoughts and me

3 am rough against my skin insomnia

frown lines
I carve away
my anxiety

self-mutilation
the scars you see
the ones you don't

burrowing undercover the screams and h**owls**

piling up
beneath the bed
nightmares

stepping b(a)ckwards
        (ni)ghtly through
      (som)eone else's
labyr(in)th

flying through negative space the meditation blackbird

restless night
// //\‾‾‾/\\ \\
psychic • spiders
\\ \\/___\V/ //
weaving nightmares

ridding the psyche
of troublesome thoughts—
mindwipe

possession—
a child's toy speaks
to an empty room

crime scene tape—
the puzzle piece
edged in blood

beneath his shoe
the cloudy globe
of your eye

blood spatter
so many ways
to die

purge fluid releasing the demons

this evening
shrouded in fog...
ghostlight

scattered light
this phantom
darkness

conjoined—
my spectral twin
denies our existence

between life
a razor-thin line
and death

at the bottom
of my soul
an open grave

at the freshly dug grave
I think only of myself
jumping in

a dark mouth
swallows galaxies
sipping endlessly
through the wormhole
life is consumed

in the space
between wakefulness and sleep
tentacles

two a.m.
the void form
returns...
watch me sleep
with no eyes

night terror—
when I wake up
he's still here

instead of a halo
this one has horns—
I yell at the kids
to shut
the portal

two puncture wounds
to the chest...
her soul slides out
the great unknown
slithers in

alien waste pit
amid outgrown appendages
one severed head
"Made in the USA"
stamped on the helmet

crumpled space suit
an alien unzips
my body

in the bin
marked for recycling—
my old skin

cast-off bodies
behind the alien café
the delicacy
of freshly squeezed
human eyes

lunch date—
my lover's canines
pierce the vein

zombie diner—
a dusting of dandruff
seasons the soup

after dinner
unbuttoning
his belly

LEFTOVERS

one
cold,
rusty,
human nail
is all that remains
from yesterday's wonderful meal

another nightmare—
the window creeper feasting
on your alpha waves

quaking aspen:
myriad blinking eyes
witness the dawn

inching closer
I hear their veiled threats...
trees

red bubbles of foam
gurgle from the forest floor...
the oaks turn away

deep in conversation
I do not notice when
you absorb me

finishing her story—
the beginning stages
of decomposition

ABOUT THE AUTHOR

Julie Bloss Kelsey discovered speculative haiku in 2009, with her first science fiction haiku (scifaiku) publication in August of that year. Subsequently, she began writing haiku, tanka, kyoka, cherita, haibun, and other short forms. Her poetry has since been published worldwide, winning awards in Japan, Canada, Croatia, and the United Kingdom, in addition to the United States. Julie has served on the board of The Haiku Foundation since 2020, where she writes and edits a bi-monthly column for haiku newcomers called New to Haiku. She is currently an editor at *Frogpond*. She is the author of three prior collections of poetry: *The Call of Wildflowers* (Title IX Press, 2020), the award-winning *Grasping the Fading Light: A Journey Through PTSD* (Sable Books, 2023), and *After Curfew* (Cuttlefish Books, 2023). Julie lives in suburban Maryland with her husband, three kids, a bark-happy dachshund, and a varying number of fish. In her spare time, she likes to study natural history, wield a hot glue gun, drink iced decaf lattes, and meet new people. Connect with her on Instagram (@julieblosskelsey).